*Direct all enquiries to the publisher:*

*The RightEyedDeer Press*
*PO Box 236*
*Haliburton, ON*
*Canada K0M 1S0*

*http://therighteyeddeer.weebly.com*



***ISSN 1918-8336 The RightEyed Deer***

# CONTENTS



*Issue # 8*

# EDITORIAL

After a year of hibernation the Deer finally stirred and shook off its slumber in Spring 2011. The rejuvenated and much refreshed beast proved to be greatly invigorated after twelve months rest.

In the first editorial Doug Pugh referred to the fact that we were all amazed by both the quantity and quality of the writing which had been submitted for our consideration. Subsequent issues have continued to go from strength to strength.

The first edition of 2012 is, I believe, the strongest to date. There has once again been an embarrassment of riches, no question of scratching around for work to include - rather a case of agonising over which pieces to leave out.

We decided at the very beginning that the criteria for inclusion should be centred on the excellence of the writing. Little did we realise that we should be in the position of having to exclude work which would have graced most other publications. It has been a joy to read so much fine work and regret that we had to omit many beautiful pieces.

There is a deep debt of gratitude to many writers who feature regularly on the Write Idea forum, the consistency and quality of their writing is the backbone of the Deer, often stunningly so. I have to confess, however, that the work of new writers from all over the world has been a particular delight and, for me, a great thrill has been the work of writers who work in genres outside my personal comfort zone who inspire me with a perspective and language which I should never in my wildest dreams be able to emulate. The work of Tom Pescatore in this edition is a case in point.

The Deer is still, of course, a fledgling publication and there is much to be done before it achieves major recognition. This will not happen quickly but I am confident that it will happen over time if we continue to progress as we have done to date, meanwhile it is a publication of which we can all be justifiably proud and one in which we can delight and develop.

I cannot conclude without paying tribute to the other members of the editorial team. Doug has been an inspiration and has worked tirelessly to ensure that we succeed even to the point of producing the artwork for this edition; Jesse who has worked with Doug to ensure the best short fiction; John who I believe will make a major contribution to the presentation of the Deer; and my particular thanks to Mandy for leading the way as joint poetry editor and for putting up with me.

An excellent start to the New Year and I trust a happy year to all.

***Mike Noakes***

# MAPMAKER

don't colour it blue
use brown and grey
follow the path of silt
that pillows the walls
of old docks and quays
and don't be fooled
by the empty plots
of abandoned land
or sprawling suburbia
my home town river
still kisses the exotic
mouth to full mouth
where the estuary
meets the North Sea

*Julie Corbett*

# ABSTINENCE

Paris stood alone on the mountain and three goddesses flew though his fantasy, three images each waiting for the gift, the fruit in his hand, each offering arousing promise to his craggy aspect. But Paris could have no goddess; only their voices could touch him, even the echoes withheld. Paris ate the apple; he bit deep and the seeds fell out, desires sown on stone, thwarting god and nature with only rocks to reprove.

# THERE FOR EVERYONE TO SEE

Claire's head was thrown back in laughter. Her new husband had his arm round her waist; his mouth at her ear telling her a filthy joke. She glowed warm with happiness, despite the chill October day.

Dressed in vivid green, her best friend, Kate, looked on, amazed at how truly beautiful Claire looked; how James leaned in so intimately, how content they were to be united.

Twenty-one years later, looking at the photograph that had immortalised that moment for ever, Claire smiled as she remembered what James had said.

"You can see the connection even then," her mother commented.

Claire was in a daze of bereavement, after days of sorting through paper and possessions. It took a moment before her mother's words registered and she realised what was held in her hand.

"What do you mean by connection?" Claire asked. "He was being very rude." She smiled at the memory. "It's lovely to have such a great picture of the three of us together."

"He's looking directly at her, see?"

And suddenly she did see – her husband, on their wedding day, gazing at her best friend while whispering in his bride's ear. And Kate gazing back at him.

"How did I never see this? This picture was on the piano the whole time."

"Darling, why do you think they were in the car together?"

Tears rolled down Claire's face. As realisation dawned, she pushed the photograph into the shredder.

***Elizabeth Donnelly***

# THINKING MAYBE 1,2,3 TURN THE COLD WATER DOWN

Is this what we do now,
sit and stare and grow old forgetting?
I can feel the lines on my face each time
you close your eyes and say
you're tired... the world outside
is blasting colors at our windows
but we are here wanting to grow up
wanting to die
I don't get it
sleeping soundly for another day
so what? the sun comes up and
we can see and superman gains the
ability to fly, he's younger than we are at
75, he may last forever on the page... the guy against
the window tries to help me, I'm telling
the teller-ticket-taker someone left a phone,
I give it to her knowing she's just gonna
sell the fucking thing, but there's nothing I
can do, I could take it, steal it, destroy it
I don't get it,
what do they want leaving things on the seats?
herded out of buses, the wrong buses,
idiot buses, he's got thick glasses/Obama beret,
I die each time I see that
Days Inn, with the no cars
and pretend continental breakfast savior...
when am I going to blow it up?
I dunno, I'd like to soon, but there's no
explosives left in a dying world,
just us, frown on our faces in the shower
leaning against the tiles afraid to pee,
thinking, ah the hell with it, then taking a
breath and starting all over again

***Tom Pescatore***

# MEMORIES

Remember when I sat on that
couch in Hyattsville, MD, I all
but owned the first floor and the
shower in the corner past the kitchen
with its black ants crawling up the
wall and getting wet by the hanging
shower head--crawling on my clothes,
sliding into the sink--those fucking ants,
I couldn't save them and they
followed me into that small green
tiled foggy cell;
Remember how I'd watch them
uneasily while undressing, like the slugs
slithering across my kitchen floor in
dead-winter, thinking, "What the fuck am
I doing here?"

***Tom Pescatore***

# YOUR BODY LIES WITH BIRDS

And in that woven painted dream
You spoke to me in silver words
Softly first, but then a scream
And in that woven painted dream
I followed you across the seam
To where your body lies with birds
And in that woven painted dream
You spoke to me in silver words

I followed you across the seam
To where your body lies with birds
Where beaks and blackened eyes still gleam
I followed you across the seam
To where your blood now feeds the stream
That babbles on your silver words
I followed you across the seam
To where your body lies with birds

*Jesse Gadsby*

# MOUNTAIN CLIMBING UNDER THE INFLUENCE

You were always going to be a hike. And, at first, I was well out of shape; rigorous training required. You seemed worth training for. In fact, there was never a moment when I could see another option. In my albatross mind, you were it. I wooed you and showered... no, bathed you in gifts: Dom Pérignon and David Austin roses. And yet I barely got my hiking boots on.

It soon became clear you were a marathon, my heart constantly switched to rapide; a thin layer of sweat could appear from nowhere — like condensation on a wine glass. I was always on edge, wondering what more I could do. Like the time at Royale when five out of six courses were tres horribles. And later that evening, Les Miserable garnered a similar response. Even after a private fireworks show, your panties remained chained to your slender hips. To you, I was yawn-inducing. Yet I soldiered on.

How strange it was that on a Saturday afternoon, while I read by a rain-spattered window, you approached me, naked and wet from the shower. A hunger I'd never seen before. At once, I was Edmund Hillary proceeding with great haste up the mountain. We moved swiftly across pebbles and rocks, and then through boulders. But, upon reaching the peak, everything changed. My skin recoiled and my eyes fell shut. I rolled over and you reached out for me. And I wondered what Edmund Hillary felt upon reaching the summit.

# COTTAGE OPENING

First guest of the year,
he helps replace pallets
that waves have lifted
from the dock last month,
after the ice went out.

Two she has recovered,
and a third they look for,
finding it before elevenses,
half a mile downwind
in sheltered Turtle Bay —

At brutal noon they labour
shirtless over granite boulders
to erect a dry-stone wall
around her columbines
and early plantain lilies.

Before yard arm time
they set the boat lift in its place,
and swim, the water only bearable,
her nipples blue, his scrotum tight.
Whip-poor-wills tonight.

*E. Russell Smith*

# FAULKNER'S ISLAND

Hot for any exertion,
but I have agreed
to helm the dinghy,

boom too low to duck
when going about, jib sheets
slack on either tack,

my mate more ornamental
on the foredeck
than useful in the cockpit.

After an hour in irons,
we're moored at last,
sails struck and stowed.

We strip to swim, but sprawl
face up on the dock, too tired
to fall into the tepid lake.

A warm wind roars in old pines
splayed overhead in
pallid sky and white-hot sun.

O! for the promised rain!
We will swim in the night air,
cool as two feet under.

*E. Russell Smith*

# DONE DEAL

When Harry Mac came in that evening there was a shine in his eyes like he was lit from within.

He slapped his book down on the bar and called to Jeff who was sorting banknotes at the till.

' Jeff,' he said, tapping the book with his finger,' I've hit the mother lode. Get these sad fuckers a drink on me.'

He slid a credit card across, pulled out a stool and gave us that smile of his.

'So how's business for you boys?'

He knew how it was. Order books unthumbed. Appointments cancelled, doors left unanswered. It was classic Harry to be closing deals while the rest of us were just about closing down.

No one had been on the road so long or done it with such style – black suit, silk shirt, gold watch, shoes of Italian leather. The shirts he was famous for – Harry boasted he carried just two, one on his back and one for drying overnight in his room.

We got hammered on Harry that night. Jeff locked the place down and the tequilas kept coming, Harry at the centre of it all with his jokes and stories.

It was me who found him in the morning, flat on the bed with his jacket buttoned and jaw hanging slack. Beside him some pills and the order book open on the first page. Empty, as clean as the day it was printed. At the window his shirt turned slowly in the breeze.

***Connal Vickers***

# LOOSE ENDS

It was November when I noticed
you'd colour-coded the clothes pegs
in a row across the top of the red vinyl bag
that hangs on the nail behind the front door.

Maybe it was an end-of-season
tidying-up kind of thing. The winter coming on.
The damp. The pointlessness of hanging on the line
kind of thing.

When December came you said
you'd read about a pill so full of vitamins
and minerals there'd be no need for food.
One-a-day would do. There'd be no messy

cooking, no plates, no pans, no washing up
but for now you'd microwave the occasional
Tesco ready-meal from the boxes arranged
in alphabetical order in the freezer.

By January there were only your shoes. Marching
two-by-two step by the locked front door. I found you
in the wardrobe neatly pressed in your best.
Shirt and tie from M&S.

*Marilyn Francis*

# THE SEASONS AND THE SLANTS

I live my life inside my patio window.
It's here, at my business desk I slip
into my own warm pajamas and slippers-
seek Jesus, come to terms
with my own cross and brittle conditions.
Outside, winter night turns to winter storm,
the blue jay, cardinal, sparrows and doves
go into hiding, away from the razor whipping winds,
behind willow tree bare limb branches-
they lose their faces in somber hue.
Their voices at night abbreviate
and are still, short like Hemingway sentences.
With this poetic mind, no one cares
about the seasons and the slants
the wind or its echoes.
I live my life inside my patio window.

# PICTURE, CAP AND GOWN

Cap and gown
history major,
minor in math-
graduation under
the maple tree,
bright red leaves,
but the times don't show it;
a full face grins.
There's a shadow
below your nose
above your lips,
it settles into
a gray mixed day.
You stand on farm land
with no plough in hand
or in the distance bare;
no damn cows to be seen
no red barn or damn homestead
just open acres of space,
and downed fences,
and some idle brush
blending with quill feathers
flushed within a background
of branches.
Life is a simple picture.
Life is a simple picture,
repeating with tree shadows
hovering around leaves.
Dirt background is dances freely
it is here memories are folded
into prairie wind.
You are still framed
in solid black and white,
you can't leave this space alone,
from now to your own eternity,
to your salvation or your grave.
Your whole life now has spots
and spaces behind it.
Did you grow older and have children?
Did you marry a man of the plough
or that chemist you had the brief
affair with in agricultural school?
Did the graduation certificate
rolled up in your hand
like a squashed turnip,
donut, or dead sea scroll
faded by moisture or sun
wind cursed with sand?
I pull down your life
and frame it here
like a staged curtain
hand full of future,
present, passed, and pasted
in a space dimension of
3" x 5" tucked beneath
a simple footnote of time.

# BEST TASTED COLD

Across the square a lick of wind flicked leaves and scraps into the air. She watched them flurry and curl and fall back to the pavement – leaves, crisp packets, a torn envelope, paper bleached from too long in the sun.

She sat at a table in pale city sunlight and stirred her espresso as the scraps settled down. An attractive woman, tailored and groomed, high heels crossed beneath her chair, nails crimson immaculate. She tapped the spoon against her cup and laid it on the saucer, liking the sound it made – the sound of coffee being taken, of all being well with the world.

From a bag slung on her chair she brought out an envelope and laid it on the table as if setting a place for a guest. She sipped at the coffee, lowered her cup to the saucer and composed her arms.

After a time she saw a beige taxi making its way up one of the lanes that led to the square. It stopped and a man climbed out, bent to pay the driver, said something and laughed at the reply. He shook the driver's hand and walked towards her. Mr Personality, she thought. Everyone's nice guy.

His stride was long, his posture tall, the suit moving smoothly with his body. Whatever else he is, she thought, he does look good in suits.

"Angie, how are you?" He bent for a kiss. She presented her cheek.

"You're late."

"I know." He looked around, raised a hand for service.

"Nice suit – expensive was it?"

He sat back, adjusted the jacket. "You've done alright out of me."

Behind him the leaves swirled again and settled. Her nails caught sunlight as she leaned forward to tap the envelope.

"That's for you."

"Ah come on babe I –"

"Don't call me babe. I'm not your babe."

"Ange," he fixed his eyes on hers. "Let's not do this. It won't happen again. I told you."

She looked at his jaw, the wide shoulders, the certainty of his smile. Ruler of the roost. Cock in a suit. The affair was one thing – distinguished only by it being the one she finally caught him at – but it is his talking she will never forget.

It was good in public, bad behind doors – badgering, arrogant and laced with sarcasm and sneering contempt. Worst of all was the line he used with such smug pleasure whenever there were things to discuss: 'Let's see if you can figure it out for yourself shall we?'

She sat back in her chair, the aluminium back cold through her jacket. "Sign the papers Cliff – I've got things to do."

"I hear you've been shopping for lingerie."

"Like you're ever going to see it. You going to open that envelope?"

A waitress brought him coffee and iced water. He ran his eyes down her legs, said, "Thanks darling, keep the change."

"Cliff I've been here long enough. You know the deal. We do this now or I go."

He sat back, loosened his jacket, cocked his head to one side and grinned. "Ange, c'mon. It doesn't have to be this way." He moved forward, laid his arms across the table. "There's a lot of fun we could still be having."

"In your dreams. You've blown it." She grabbed the envelope, slid back her chair and stood up. "We'll do this the hard way then."

"Whoa. No, no. Okay, I'm sorry. Again."

"Let me tell you one last time Cliff. This is simple. Even for you. Sign the papers and I'll tell you where it's hidden. Fuck me around just one more minute and my lawyer will suck you so dry you can't spit."

His shoulders tensed and he sat up straight, his eyes down like a poker player heading for a big fall. He opened the envelope, flicked through the papers without reading them, signed on the line and flipped it back across the table.

"There you go. You've got it. Now give me the keys."

She laid a key ring on the table. A badge set in leather, prancing horse with its hooves punching the air.

"It's parked underground at the Arndale. It's been there a while so it might cost you."

"You spiteful bitch. Why there? The place is fucking huge. What level is it on?"

She picked up the papers, looked him in the eyes and said through cool painted lips: "Let's just see if you can figure that out for yourself shall we?"

***Connal Vickers***

# THE RUSTED WRECK AT BARON CLIFF

I have seen two dead bodies in my life. I am not speaking of mangled chickens dropped by intruding foxes, or hacked up pigs at the slaughterhouse. Nor do I mean stiff field mice that failed to find shelter when winter hit. Animal carcasses are commonplace. What I am referring to goes beyond a partially-decapitated rabbit caught in a trap. Indeed, these were the genuine article: empty, pallid humans.

I seldom meet people in my isolated farmland life. And I certainly did not meet these two people while they lived. But in death, I have come to know them. Not only the intricacies of their faces, which often fill my night time dreaming, but the circumstances leading to their death and, in fact, everything that came before.

Upon locating the bodies and disposing of the remains, I took to town for the first time in almost half a century and spent a year of my life investigating the two departed strangers. I had to pin souls to these vessels, if only for my own peace of mind. To completely cleanse my conscience, I needed to understand them. So I learned everything from their names, to which side of the bed they slept on and even their dental history. But ultimately, I learned of the pain and fury that passion can bring.

I discovered the first body exactly where it was supposed to be. After carefully making my way down Baron Cliff, and across the narrow beach, I arrived at the shipwreck, shovel in hand. And there he sat straight-legged, his body bound to the rib of a rusted hull. His feet were bare to the elements, which had caused them to flake away. Toenails were nonexistent. I looked him up and down. Knowing I wasn't ready to touch him, I started digging.

His name was James Unwinn: twenty-seven, married, a watchmaker. He had no children to speak of, despite him and his wife trying fruitlessly for years. A neighbour has since told me that James was the essence of handsomeness. "He had a face that radiated," she said. But what haunts me is a very different face; a face with eyeballs pecked out by gulls and flesh rotting at the jaw revealing sand-peppered bone. A face that gasped for air before drowning in the sea below Baron Cliff.

It was a letter from my estranged sister that took me to Baron Cliff. Her letter arrived weeks after James had met his end and was written in a manic fashion, as though she only had minutes to compose it. And though I had not spoken to her in years, her words now echo with me every day, just as they did when I looked down on James' body.

*I've done something unforgivable. Killed a man. I left him to die. He's chained to the shipwreck at Baron Cliff. I expect Nature had her way with him. Over and over. I need to tell someone the truth. To repent.*

What had she done? And why had it taken something like this to bring her back into my life?

*They also say I killed a woman. But I only slashed her ankles. I'm carrying his child, and I told her so. I told her where her husband would be. If she truly loved him she would weather the storm and rescue him. Seems she didn't love him, just as he never loved me.*

*I will be executed tomorrow. Forgive me.*

The storm she wrote of was unrelenting and lasted more than a week. Whipping rain, thunder and hurricane-winds menaced the entire region. I cannot imagine the pain one would endure if exposed to such conditions. But I know what it looks like.

After burying James the best I could, I made my way back up the cliff and walked through the grassy fields above. I had travelled less than half a mile when I saw Evelyn Unwinn outstretched on the grass, her hands clawing at the earth. Sliced tendons left a trail of black blood on her white feet. Evelyn's head was pointed firmly toward the cliff, her chin coming to rest parallel to the ground. Her face was peeling off, lips were all but removed and hair flapped in the breeze, so utterly windswept.

*If she truly loved him she would weather the storm...*

Later, upon flipping her face-up into a grave, I noticed for the first time, in her hand, a rusted dagger, as cast-iron as the sword in the stone.

***Mitchell Noel Kelly***

## MONOSPECTIVE

More known as one of our fiction editors rather than as an artist, Doug has a pretty broad range of talents. 'Equally bad at all of them,' he will joke, 'but passionate about expression.'

Doug's loss of vision in one eye just a few years back (an elusive auto-immune problem) gives him a few difficulties in perspective sometimes, but he tries to regard it as another angle.

'Like most things, it's purely shape and light. Then you just splash on a bit of imagination, a dash of brave colour and maybe a rash belief that it all makes sense.'

Known locally for his poetry and his black eye patch, Doug lives in 'Cottage country' in Ontario, a land filled with lakes, trees and a dazzling artistic community. Haliburton Highlands is one of the lowest income areas in Canada but draws in swathes of tourists for its rich art scene, the subject of several 'Tours' as collectors visit the various studios.

'There is inspiration in so many layers here, the people, the environment, nature. There is no place to start except right where you are, right now ... you just have to say something in whatever form it takes.'

Doug was voted 'Fiction Writer of the Year' on The Write Idea forum, something that he says was probably the most humbling accolade of his creative career to date. He has had poetry and fiction printed in national newspapers and magazines on both sides of the Atlantic and further, but has yet to venture very far with his art.

You can find out more about Doug's art and the Haliburton art scene at these sites:

www.haliburtonarts.on.ca

www.madeinhaliburton.ca

(launching in March 2012)

Douglas Pugh

# HANGING ON

Who would think something I learned so long ago would now help me cope with this loss?

Lesson: When you hang on by your fingernails day after day, you toughen your muscles. Later when you don't have to clutch so desperately, the strength remains, only you can use it however you choose. That applies to mental and emotional muscles too, not just physical ones.

I first saw her in the parking lot where the bus was to pick us up for the trip to summer camp in Muskoka. I was instantly mesmerized by her long blond hair, sparkling blue eyes, and flawless complexion. She even made the ugly yellow T-shirt that said 'Camp Kanandaga – Staff' look good.

I was also wearing one since I was to be one of five Leaders-In-Training. As I later found out, the others were former campers. As I also found out, my Life Guard qualifications were uncommon and probably part of the reason an outsider was accepted. There was no pay, only free attendance, but my parents promised me the money they would save on food. Since they frequently complained about how much I ate, I assumed that would be substantial.

It was a Co-ed camp, rare in those days, and probably one of the reasons Ronny Barker from my Grade Eight class also applied. Before the interviews, he speculated non-stop about the girls we might meet. He's a jerk and it probably showed because he wasn't hired. I wasn't disappointed at all. I was looking forward to meeting new people once high school started in September.

Being cool far outweighs family values when you're thirteen, so I told Dad not to bother hanging around after he dropped me off. Our ancient rusty car was a major embarrassment. When my older brother drove it, he avoided the steep, busy hill on Parkhill Avenue unless I was along to pretend to the line of drivers behind us that I was looking for an address and that's why we were going so slowly.

She was already there. Most of the kids waiting for the bus were with family and despite their excitement, relatively controlled. However, one small group without parents was tormenting another boy. Somehow, they had gotten his toothpaste and one was exclaiming over the Crestworms he was making on the pavement while the others restrained the victim.

She stared at me. I realized her eyebrows were raised because I was wearing a staff shirt so I resisted the urge to check my fly. "Enough of that," I barked in a commanding voice. Fortunately, it didn't break and they stopped. Try being the voice of authority in a squeaky falsetto.

After that, it made sense that we sit together on the bus. I used Ronny as a model of how not to act. I mostly asked questions, since my sister once told me girls didn't want to hear self-bragging all the time. Besides, I was always concerned about my voice breaking. I was pleasantly surprised to discover she was only a few months older than me, a former camper returning as another LIT.

At the camp, we stood beside the bus, me catching luggage dropped from the roof-racks. As I stood looking up to avoid being squashed, I said she could show me around, picturing moonlit, hand-in-hand strolls. I didn't notice the other bus arrive.

When I caught the next duffel bag and turned to the growing pile beside me, I discovered she had moved to the newly-arrived bus and was clenched in an embrace with a guy who had just exited. He too was another LIT, and apparently a romance between them had developed the previous summer. He lived in Toronto and camp offered them a chance to be together again.

I was devastated, but I had no time to lick my wounds as I was thrown into the cauldron of kids, cabin assignments, and lost luggage.

Not knowing anyone at camp had seemed like a good thing at first, but after that shattering experience, it wasn't so attractive. Even Ronny would have listened to my lament, despite being an ass. But I discovered no matter how badly your heart aches, the world doesn't stop for your grief, and you can keep going long after you think you can't.

I learned the 'T' in LIT stands for 'toil', not just 'training'. When a camper heaves after Parents' Day because they took him to town for candy and ice-cream, the counsellor takes the kid to the infirmary; the LIT cleans up. On cold mornings, the swimming instructor sits on a picnic table on shore calling instructions while the LIT is turning blue in the lake with the kids.

The next few weeks felt like years as I was confronted by my loss every day. However, eventually the sessions when I saw them together when all groups shared the Craft Hall weren't quite as bad, and I actually started to look forward to meal-time in the communal Dining Hall. Nothing before had ever kept me from appreciating food.

Then Week Seven brought Robbie. These days, I think they would label him Bipolar, but back then, he was simply a problem kid. I quickly became his keeper, as the cabin counsellor declared he would watch the others so I could focus on Robbie.

I was bigger and could run faster. So when Robbie ran, which was his response to every minor frustration, I would catch him. We were always close enough to camp that I could carry the struggling, swearing kid back, which would probably result in a lawsuit nowadays but was accepted without question back then.

It wasn't until a few years later that I realized the physical side of that situation was actually the least draining part. The emotional demands had been much worse. Later still, I understood I was able to cope because I had been continuously confronted by her presence. When you hang on day after day like I had done, you build up strength.

So here's the advice. Get through the hard times by reminding yourself you're building muscles that will remain after the pain diminishes. Later you'll be able to use that strength however you want. It'll be a welcome remnant.

I remind myself that's what's happening when I awake to the empty pillow beside me.

***Bob Smith***

# THE LONGEST NIGHT

I

deep winter
waiting
for her last breath

bare trees
reflected
in her wasted frame

snow-heavy sky
the air thick
with things left unsaid

II

lights out
the pain in her eyes
vanishes

a blizzard
covers the tracks
of the hearse

in the silence
of her passing
I make tea

*Tracy Davison*

# SHIMMERING

Her silver swimsuit shimmered as she came out of the hotel and walked over to the pool. She stood there, looking down at the water.

"Zeffie!" I called over.

"Do I know you?" she called back, shadowing her eyes with a hand.

"Let's just say that I'm a poetical bird of uncertain identity."

"Like a sea-swallow?" she said, coming closer.

"I said 'uncertain'."

"Is that you, Mark?"

"Could be," I said, "I thought you were too broke to get out of town?"

"I took a loan to clean up my finances.  You coming in?"

We splashed around a bit then sat by the pool, small-talking, our feet dangling over the edge. After a while she began to shiver.

"Hey, let's get you into some warm clothes," I said, "Then get a coffee down your neck."

"Sure," she said, "Though it won't do any good.  The cold is coming from the inside."

We headed into the hotel.

"Meet you down at Reception in ten minutes?" I said.

"Make that fifteen."

We walked along the beach towards the harbour, paddling a bit as we went.  Bronze brutes watched us all the way.

"Doesn't it bother you?" I asked.

"Doesn't what bother me?"

I jerked a thumb behind us.

"Oh, no," she said, "I can shut them out when I want to and let them in when I'm feeling low."

"But the crudity of it," I said.

"You just don't like people," she said, "That's your problem.  Richard told me."

We walked in silence for a while.

"Say, you don't fancy me, do you?" she asked.

"Of course not!"

"Good, because that'd be a problem."

"There's no chance of it," I said.

At the harbour we both took a coffee.

"Isn't Richard with you?" she asked.

"He was. He's gone off exploring some of the islands. He might even have gone over to Troy. You alone?"

"Yes. I only managed to get the loan last minute. All my friends had already taken off. So, he isn't coming back then?"

"Oh, you know Ricky. If he finds a girl, he'll stay put a day or two before moving on. Maybe he'll pass by on his way back."

We took another coffee.

"Are you writing anything at the moment? Richard said you wrote poetry."

"I've given it up."

"Why?"

"I'm not in the mood. Besides, I never was any good."

"What will you do instead?"

"Ricky says I should take up technical writing. He's pulling in five grand a month and he's only just started."

We walked out on one of the piers and looked at the boats.

"They seem so pure," she said.

I looked up at the sun.

"I should have brought my sunglasses out with me."

She squinted upwards.

"Won't it ever stop?"

"What, the sun? Not for a long time yet."

She shivered.

"Still cold?"

"Like I said, it's coming from the inside."

Back at the hotel we arranged to eat later.

"Listen, do you have an e-mail address or mobile for Ricky or something?"

"We're Facebooking."

"What, like right now, while he's island-hopping?"

"Yes."

"Tell him I'm here, can't you?"

"Are you chasing him?"

"No. It's over."

"You two dated?"

"All last term. He didn't tell you?"

"No."

"Well, he likes to be secretive. See you for dinner."

"Should we eat here?"

"No, let's hit town."

Town was overcrowded. So, we walked out and up to the point.
"I managed to get hold of Ricky," I said.
"And?"
"He says he'll be back in three or four days. He asked how long you were staying. How long are you staying?"
"Six weeks."
"Jesus! That must have been some loan."
"It was."

I ate lamb, Zeffie had red snapper. After dinner we sat around drinking, waiting for the sun to go down. It was getting a bit chilly.
"You cold?" I asked.
"No," she smiled, "You?"
"Just a touch. What do you say we go down into the town?"

The next few days we spent together. We lazed by the pool. I read Berryman, Browning and Byron to her. I was working my way through the Bs.
"Let's get out of here," she said on the third day.
"What do you mean?"
"Take in a tourist site or something; I'm tired of just waiting around for that ..."

I hired a moped and we rode out to the Petrified Forest. It was inland and it took a couple of hours to get there. As soon as we left the coastal rode we began to bake slowly. Once there it was hard to get off the bike and walk into the plantation. There was hardly any shade. We walked down into the forest, then up and around it. We tried to take an interest but it was so desolate.
"I guess that's why they call it the Petrified Forest," Zeffie said.

We were starving so we headed over to a town on the other side of the island as it was closer, even though it meant a hell of along ride back to the hotel. We ate in a restaurant on the beach. I tried to pick up some of Sappho's poetry but they only had volumes in Greek or German.
"We'd better head back," I said.
"Let's wait until the sun dips further," she said.
"I don't want to risk driving through the dark; I haven't even checked the lights on that thing."
"At least wait until it gets cooler."

We paddled in the sea a little then went back into the village. I picked up the Sappho in Greek.
"But you can't read Greek, what's the point?"
"I don't know, we're tourists aren't we, it's better than picking up a key-ring. Want to take a beer?"
"No. Let's head back."
"Okay," I said, "Ricky might be in."
"He's coming today?"
"Maybe. Are you that eager to see him?"
"Not especially. It ended badly. I just wanted to tell him no hard feelings."
"He seems to think you want to get back."
She laughed, a touch harshly.

Richard got in next morning. He woke me up.

"Rise and shine!"

"What the ..."

"Let's do breakfast, you lazy oaf. Where's Zeffie?"

I told him her room number then climbed into the shower. That ride back had really done me in.

They were already eating when I got down. I took a coffee, some orange juice and a slice of marmalade toast.

"Not much of an appetite," Richard said.

"I don't know how you guys can eat in this heat."

We went out to the pool. Zeffie had a black swimsuit on today.

"What happened to the silver one?" I asked.

"Oh, you like that, do you?"

"I guess."

Richard and Zeffie splashed around a bit but the fun was forced. She went up to shower and take a lie down.

"I don't get it," Ricky said.

"Get what?"

"That she doesn't want to get back together. I mean, what did she come out here for?"

"Her friends took off. I think she said South America. Maybe we were the closest, you know ..."

"I just don't get it."

"Well, you don't want to get back with her anyway, do you?"

"I didn't think so but, well, maybe I'm bored. Where are the girls?"

"It was your idea to come here."

"Is she dating anybody out here?"

"No."

"Are *you* chasing her?"

"Absolutely not."

"Strange. To think I was just about to go over to Troy as well. You still heading back Saturday?"

"Maybe."

"Only maybe?"

"I had this idea for some poems; maybe I'll stick around and see if they work out."

Ricky took off the next day. Zeffie came down to the pool in her silver swimsuit. I started on the first of my poems: *Shimmering*.

# KNOXVILLE: A THEME-WEAVE

*inspired by Barber's "Knoxville: Summer of 1915"*

A cradling rock
houses the disguise
as a closet case
and an abandoned case
recite a dream
of a supportive family
in one seeming calm town
in a hinged world

partly mounted
by a bustle
that is not of 1915
but masquerades as well
as such.

Electric sputter
plays Cassandra
although it precedes
the wartime marvel
of being mystified
by cricket song

until one note
announces by its thinness
its height
and dew hovers
resists falling
also cheating

as the voice contours the quietude
that slipped in, all the same,
after the disquietude.

What is
the sorrow in quilts?
We know, almost,
and almost hear
a Hebrew benediction.

It tries to hold
against the swirl
behind the stars
sinister winds
and chance mumming fortune
even as "well-beloved" itself is anxious.
But what happens?
What happens?
"Nothing at all."

But

    yet

the begged question
is stated
not asked
and that
crepuscular last word

telescopes yards
wars
beasts
tessiturae

into a sleep that smiles
draws in
does not draw away
feints . . .

iron has still entered
and tolls
in the last
high chime.

***Maude Larke***

# MOVEMENTS

I.

I did my walking

on the dusty and grassy parts only

a reverse wake of grasshoppers

flowed away in front of me

I was thinking of how

the same road and the same direction

had been both walking home and walking away

II.

I was sitting in a cramping seat

feeling my buttocks forming corners as we rose

an intermittent rainbow striped the wing

the white arc had gone with the ground

I was wondering when

this squealing track of air

would be homeward and down instead

III.

I lay pressed belly to side

against her as she breathed her sleep in like pain . . .

I felt that my heart

would do nothing but run the way it was

until I could lie like that again

*Maude Larke*

# THE BUGGER BROTHERS

There is a stiff breeze blowing across Roker Beach as I plod through the soft sand towards the water. Everything, and I mean everything, seems to be getting into my eyes: the overbright sun, the sand, even the sea spray.

I've been too long in this town. It's time to get out; most people do as soon as they've finished their degree. They either move back home or move on. What's kept me here? Surely just some kind of paralysis, I guess.

I gaze out at the North Sea. The Faroe Islands are out there somewhere, Norway, Iceland, the States ... Jimmy comes running out of the sandhills. I sense him before I see him. Or maybe I catch, faintly, his words because, as I turn, it is clear that he has been shouting at me though I couldn't hear anything above the wind, the crashing of the waves and the cawing of the gulls. Finally, he comes up to me.

"All right, Jimmy?" I ask.

"Didn't you hear what I was saying?"

"No."

He takes in a couple of lungfuls of air.

"The Bugger brothers are in town."

I think about that for a moment, it isn't a pleasant thought.

"So?"

"So, they'll murder you, you better get out."

The Bugger brothers isn't their real name, I'm not quite sure how they'd picked up the nick but it gives you an idea of their reputation.

"Look, it's not as though I've done anything wrong, Jimmy."

"You just finished with their sister!"

"Well, I'm not the first!"

"Maybe not but you might just be the last. The others hadn't gotten engaged to her, had they?"

Jimmy takes in a few more lungfuls of air.

"It was Frank, the barman down The Grail, who told me. He also told me that Danny was held overnight by cops last year on suspicion of rape. You never told me that?"

Well, he was right there, I hadn't.

"Frank reckons that's why Danny left town and went to stay with his brother in London."

I sigh.

"Look, Danny is no rapist. The cops grabbed him late one evening and spent the night trying to beat a confession out of him. They didn't, though they broke an arm and three ribs trying."

"Jesus!"

"In the morning they booked the real rapist and let Danny go, I think they even apologized to him."

"Apologized! He should have sued them!"

"He said it was fair enough, that he would have done the same thing himself. 'I've got a sister, myself,' he'd said to them."

It seemed a bit unfortunate, that. Not him having a sister but me recalling that line he'd used to the cops.

I thought of Derek, I'd always got on better with Derek. He had been very hospitable that time Jeannette and I had visited him in London. He introduced us to a pretty well-known pop duo. Derek played bass, used to jam with the guitarist. He also took us down the King's Road, seemed to know just about everybody.

"He seems a lot mellower than he used to be," I'd said.

"Well, he can't beat up the whole of London, can he?" had been Jeannette's comment.

One day, down the Tube waiting for one of those huge lifts to take us above ground, just Derek and I, he turned to me and said:

"I'm glad things finally seem to be working out for my sister. Take good care of her."

I thought it odd. I mean, his way of expressing it. That he didn't say he was happy that it was working out for *us*.

An elderly neighbour of Jimmy's walks by dragging a sausage dog.

"Is Negropontus, all right, Mrs L?" Jimmy asks.

"Oh yes, everything's just hunky dory, thank-you."

"Then why isn't he walking?" Jimmy insists.

She looks back at her dog and smiles.

"He tires so easily these days; it might have something to do with the change in the weather. So, Jimmy, I hear that Danny and Derek Bagely are back in town?"

"That's right, Mrs L."

"On account of the wedding, I take it?"

"The wedding was cancelled last week," Jimmy says.

"Oh, dear ..."

Mrs L bends down and pats her dog. Negropontus opens an eye, closes it again.

"Well, it's very nice of them to come up; Jeannette'll need all the support she can get. This sort of thing can ... can ... *unhinge* a girl."

"Yes," says Jimmy.

"Wasn't it some young man from the University who she was engaged to?"

"I'm not sure, Mrs L," Jimmy says, eyeing me nervously.

"I think it must have been. I don't think any of our boys would behave like that, breaking engagements, I mean. She should have chosen you, Jimmy!"

Jimmy barks out a laugh. Negropontus opens both eyes wide, slowly closes them again.

"Well ..." Jimmy doesn't quite know what to say.

"You used to get on so well together when you were younger ..."

"We was only kids, Mrs L."

"Still it would have been better than a student type. Well, we'd better see about getting home, hadn't we Neg?"

I know dogs can't smile but it does seem as though Negropontus manages a grin.

She passes by. Negropontus dark-eyes us, growling low all the while.

"You'd better high-tail it out of town," Jimmy says, "why not visit your sister down in Ripon for a few days, until they go."

"Nah ... I mean ..."

"I'm serious, mate. Look, I'll drive you there. Right now. I'll just go get the car."

"Oh, all right then," I say.

"Meet you back at your place in half-an-hour. And remember, the Bugger brothers have beaten up just about every male in this town."

"You managed to escape, Jimmy."

"No, I didn't, mate, no I didn't."

"What do you mean?"

He looks like he doesn't know whether he is going to stay or go.

"What do you mean, Jimmy?"

He's struggling with something.

"Remember when you were first going out with Jeannette?"

"Of course I do!"

"Remember she was getting those phone calls and nobody knew who was making them?"

"Yes."

There's an awkward pause. Then it comes out.

"Well, it was me."

"Jesus, Jimmy, you've got to be kidding?"

"I meant to say something, *really I did*, but every time I opened my mouth, nothing came out. I just sort of froze. I mean, I wasn't making dirty phone calls or anything ..."

I look at Jimmy. *The heavy breather*. The guy who had caused so much grief to Jeannette in our early days. I'd got mad myself many times. I'd called down the phone; I'd said that the police were tracing the call. But they went on and on, those calls, until they suddenly stopped.

"Danny caught up with me, don't ask how he found out but he did. He broke my nose and said that if he didn't know my family, he'd have killed me."

"Jesus!"

"That's why I'm going to get the car, Mark, and get you out of here."

And he disappears back the way he'd come.

A young woman in a canary-yellow bikini and a man wearing Empire green trunks run down into the water. They laugh as they go in. It must be bloody freezing. I recall the evening I'd proposed to Jeannette. We'd been drinking tequila down the Labour Club. Heading back to my place, through the town hall's car park, I'd suddenly kneeled down. It had all seemed so natural and honest. Clean. It was only the next morning that I began to think that maybe it had been the alcohol that had been doing the proposing, more specifically the little worm at the bottom of the tequila bottle.

I don't go back to my place; instead I wander over to Jeannette's. The estate looks the same. The grey semi-detached houses look gloomy, despite the low October sun. It's quiet. As I near her cul-de-sac, I come across some boys playing basketball in a fenced off compound. Some smaller boys squeak by on tricycles.

As I ring the bell, the curtains flicker next door. It'll be old Mr Worthington. I used to go to the off-licence for him, pick up a six-pack and some untipped cigarettes. He didn't trust the filters. He remembered when they used to make them out of asbestos. I wave, the curtains flicker again but that's all.

She takes a while opening the door. Her hair is up.

"Very pretty," I say, pointing.

A look of shock slowly comes over her features, her eyes bulge slightly.

"What do *you* want?" she asks.

I notice that she is wearing cherry red lipstick.

"I hear your brothers are in town."

"*So*?"

She's starting to look how she did when we broke up. When she transformed from 'my Jeannette' to someone else, someone screechy, downtrodden and altogether foreign.

"Well, I thought, you know, I'd like to meet up with them. I mean, just because we're finished, you and I ..."

Her face suddenly cracks and tears start to run down her face.

"Just because we're finished ..." I repeat.

She starts to sob, convulsively. Her mascara begins to run.

"Well, I thought, that doesn't mean I can't meet up with your brothers, does it?"

She looks at me for an instant then an unearthly wailing comes up from somewhere deep within her. It's like an inhuman cry. Something primordial. I force myself to continue.

"I hate it, don't you, when couples break up and then, you know, then I can't call your mother 'mum' anymore ..."

The wailing seems to grow in volume, if that is possible.

Jeannette's mother was probably the first out of all my girlfriend's mothers who I'd got along with. One Sunday, after dinner – and Sunday dinners were obligatory – they'd shown *Sholay*, the Bollywood musical, on Channel 4. She hadn't complained when I put it on, even though it lasted about four hours.

"It's quite good," she'd said.

Of course, she washed the dishes and did the ironing while it was on, but still.

I hear a car door slam behind me. Jimmy.

"I mean, your mother and I got on like a house on fire. I still think about her roast mallard and that great chestnut sauce she used to make ..."

Jeannette slumps to her knees. I turn around, intending to tell Jimmy that there is just no way he is going to drive me down to Ripon. Only it isn't Jimmy. It's the Bugger brothers. I give them my best smile.

"All right our Danny, Derek, how's it hanging lads?"

# LYONESSE

Here on the cliffs
where the Channel begins,
if you are hushed,
ignore the importuning crows,
you may hear the bells
that sound beneath the sea,
the bells of Lyonesse.

And on the strand
where the Channel ends,
after the seagulls go to roost
if the tide runs still
you may hear the chant of monks
offering atonement
for the city's sin.

Inside the taverns
of the town upon the bay
the men will warn you
there never was a Lyonesse;
but this deceit
is one more mark
of the city's reputation.

It lurks beneath the waves
and draws men in
makes them forget
themselves -
it is no commonwealth
but a state
of amnesia.

***Francis Hayes***

# THE CIRCUS NEEDS ME

First I learned to juggle. Then I walked the tightrope. But the moment I had to stick my head inside the jaws of a lion, I knew something at home was amiss. My life had veered off the path of normalcy and taken a hard right past the bearded lady.

Life had seemed so easy even a year ago. My twin sons and their inept big brother, aka my husband, had not yet thrown me into the fires of Mount Doom with our smaller hobbit—the cat. My husband was still employed, my sweet thirteen-year-old twinlets had not yet become teenage liars, and my sister hadn't left her husband to have an affair with the door-to-door marriage counsellor. This was even before my massage therapist, Hans, had flown the coop. A few weeks ago I showed up to my appointment only to be greeted by a six-foot-four Swedish man dressed as a Romulan. He wasn't much of a masseuse. I wondered though, if he'd ever considered a job as a strongman.

It seemed as though every aspect of my world was deteriorating. The only thing I really clung to was our cat, Alfalfa. My husband and I had found him in the field next to our house and had adopted him into the family when he just was a kitten. We were shocked to discover that whenever anything moved, and I do mean anything, he sprouted a body wig like Diana Ross's hair in a windstorm. I had never known the true meaning of scaredy-cat until I met our little rascal. He was a source of constant amusement in our house and we loved him despite his fear of everything.

I sat now, staring at my watch, waiting for the hands to move. They seemed to take forever as they wound their way around my wrist. Then I heard a familiar voice from across the room.

"Mrs. Gregory, would you like to say something?"

I looked up and saw the daunting smile of the therapist in front of me. "No, not really."

She looked perplexed as if she hadn't expected my reply. "Are you sure? Your husband seems quite concerned with your threats of leaving. I think you should say something, whatever's on your mind."

"Well, I was just wondering how much money carneys make and if they have to pay for their own corndogs."

The room was silent. My eyes sifted through the air until they stumbled upon the man sitting beside me. His expression was hilarious. His mouth was gaped open and his eyes were in a state of disbelief.

"Honey," he said, "I don't think that's funny."

I searched my audience of two for some form of support but found none. Apparently I had stunned my audience. Even the portrait of Sigmund Freud hanging on the wall was in shock. I could see him shaking his head at me as he mentally scribbled my verbal concoction.

"Well, think about it," I continued. "They work hard too; they deserve to be paid well. Especially the Tilt-a-Whirl guys. I mean come on, how many times have they had to clean up after people—especially when they've spilled their guts all over the rides. Around and around and around and arooooouuuunndddd. That just doesn't sound like a word anymore, does it?" I laughed.

"Christine! This is ridiculous," my husband said. "I'm trying to talk to you about our marriage and all you're doing is making a joke of it," he trumpeted.

"I'm not making a joke of it. I'm simply stating the obvious. Carneys have a hard life and that's that."

Our therapist interjected. "Christine, I find it interesting that you keep referencing a job from an amusement park."

"It is interesting, isn't it? And what about the rubbermen—you know...the guys who sell balloons at the circus? I wonder what they get paid."

Our therapist stammered for a reply. I could tell she was trying to find a kind way to reconnect our derailed discourse. "I think the point your husband is trying to make is that you're avoiding the real issues in your own life. Your home life, your family life. Why don't we talk about that?"

"What's there to talk about? My life is crumbling. My husband acts like a clown. He's the one responsible for this change. Our boys need a father not a friend and that's why they get away with everything. My sister lives with us and she's not allowed to answer the door anymore because of her strange fetish with delivery men. The only member of our family that I do trust is our cat, and he's so jittery that he spends more time in the litter box than he does sleeping. So you tell me, why should I be the sane one?"

A moment passed but no words were spoken. Another moment passed. Then another.

I was not impressed. "Seriously, John," I glared at my husband, "why aren't you saying something?"

"I think your sister should move out," was all he said.

"What? *Why*?" I spewed.

"Because I don't think she's helping our situation."

"See, now I think we're getting somewhere," the therapist nodded. "John, why do you think your wife's sister isn't helping?"

This time his answer was quick. "Because *her* sister was the one who invited this whole flea circus into our house. She answered the door one day and started an affair with a magician. The infection then spread to Barnum and Bailey over here," he pointed to me.

I took offense to his comment. "Look, I'm not crazy. I just feel like you don't need me anymore and that some sort of change was needed."

"No—what you need is a straight jacket," he smiled.

"Okay, Mr. Gregory—there's no need for that," the therapist said. "Try to stay positive." I could see that her occupation was evolving as the conversation continued. Soon she would be required to referee our boxing match.

"Christine, you didn't go to clown college, you went to law school for Pete's sake. You're a civil litigation lawyer. You know all about disputes between private parties...so why are you doing this to us?"

I smiled at him. "I still do private parties, John, just in a different capacity now."

"It's not the same thing and you know it," he said.

In the back of my mind I just couldn't understand what his problem was. To me it was simple: *he* was the problem. He just didn't get what I was going through. Everything, it seemed, was being dumped onto me, and for what? So that he could go and reclaim his youth? Was he that afraid to be the disciplinarian in the family? He had given up that role to hang out with his children. What they needed was to be reprimanded now and then but no, he'd passed that job to me so that he could take the easy way out. And *I* was the crazy one? I don't think so.

My husband shook his head. "What about Toby and Sam? You know—*our children*? How do you think this is affecting them?"

My answer was curt. "I've been the responsible one since they were born. Not you. At least not since you lost your job. All you do is sit and play video games with them. They don't even leave the house anymore. Well, John, I've had enough. There's another family out there that needs me," I said as I primped my red curls with my fingers.

John looked on and shook his head. "You've lost it Christine. This is insane. You need to come home and be with your family—your *real* family."

"John's right, Christine. Your family is in turmoil now and you leaving would be devastating to them. That's why he brought you here today. You may not think that you're needed right now but that's just not true. You are the monarch of your family. Your boys look up to you."

"That's a load," I laughed. "What has my husband been telling you? Did he tell you that he misplaced my work shoes? And all my make-up?"

"I didn't misplace them. The kids and I *hid* them," he said, in a controlled voice. "And what's the difference—you found them anyway."

I lifted both legs up from the ground to gaze at my polished shoes. "That's not the point."

The therapist gasped when she looked at my feet. "Christine, why don't we go back to a more positive place? How about your children? They're teenagers now and they need their mother." She looked over at John. "But they also need their father. They already have friends at school, so if you're going to help Christine get over this hump, then you're going to have to act more responsible."

"Look at us. I *am* the more responsible one. Look at my wife—just look at her! She's lost it! Put a knife in her hand and she looks like something out of Steven King's '*IT*'!"

"Okay—if you could just refrain from name calling, that would be great," the therapist said.

"John, you just don't understand me anymore. And why should you—you're just a man!" With that I stood. The smile on my face was enough to keep me going. Gently, I smoothed the creases in my clothing.

He looked at me, his eyes now glazed over in fright. "You're not leaving! You can't leave, this is crazy!"

"No honey, it's not. Oh great, and now I'm late for work—would you look at the time! They're going to kill me if I don't get to the dunk tank by eleven."

"Mrs. Gregory, please don't leave," the therapist begged.

"C'mon," I said. "Get real! I have to go to work. Now where is my rubber chicken?"

Coyly, my husband handed me the funny fowl. He produced it from his jacket which made me see that he was getting better at hiding things from me. He stumbled pathetically for his words. "What...have...they... done...to...you?"

I turned to face the floor-length mirror in the corner of the room. All I saw was perfection. My yellow and blue striped uniform beamed bright from the light shining through the window. The tight red curls from my wig accented the smooth leather of my crimson shoes. And the chicken I now held dear accompanied the belt of coloured hanker chiefs around my waist. The giant painted smile that I wore reassured me that I was doing the right thing.

As I pulled my nose out of my pocket, I had an epiphany. I could be the best clown ever. People from far and wide would come to see me and why? Because I represent the circus.

I twirled my body to flaunt my outfit in front of the mirror. "Don't I look stunning?"

There was no response.

I turned to face the audience. "Well—don't I?"

Both patrons jumped in their seats.

"You know, I think the saddest thing in the world is a sad clown. You wouldn't want to make me sad, would you? Because I could show you the old iron-jaw trick," I stared at the man in the front row.

He shook his head in dismay. "No—I wouldn't want to do that."

"That's more like it!" My eyes brimmed with a cheerful glaze. "Now, let's get this show on the road. Ballyhoo!" No other zanies, pongers, kinkers or towners could save me.

I had finally found my way to the Big Top.

***Kara Bartley***

# A MILLION WAYS

*"A million ways to show that I love you*
*I'm going to try every one."*
*-The Nylons*

In the riverbottoms, cattails are dropping their seeds
in mangy-looking clumps,
while along the ridges, the trees,
like worn-out whisk brooms,
scratch at the gray winter sky.
A misty rain begins. It's all so dreary,
yet underground, bulbs and rhizomes
bide their time.

I want to write you a Valentine poem
with cattails, trees, cold rain
as doily cutouts on a homemade card --
signifying the dishevelment of daily life,
dust-devil swirls of mess and chaos
that make me forget
the roots of love lie waiting.

But surely the best of our love
is not tucked away like a crocus-jewel inside a velvet-lined box,
a dormant ballerina waiting for the lid to be lifted
to dance to "Oh what a beautiful morning."

Instead, like the glitter the kids spilled on the craft table
that soon was seen on hands, dishes, faces, carpets,
our love is dispersed in glimmerings --
cattail fluff lifted in the wind,
or that wintery day when the ragged tree-line
puts on its shawl of tattered red lace
as the maples bud.

Something of the glitter, the fluff, the lace,
abides within and through the mundane and messy,
and grows each year
into the scattered riches of a million ways.

*Amelia Williams*

**I**

Words
Are so quick in you already
you make them dance,
punning, throwing your head back to laugh.

Words
are quills, already, clattering,
arrayed to fend off
the least slight, real or imagined.

Slender,
greengold, tall and smooth
you glow, wiry, electric,
orbiting your own body like a probability cloud.

Tired, you refuse
sleep, lose track of your position in space,
bump yourself and inflict
accidental blows as energy collapses into itself, the rim
of the volcano crumbling.

When I come to shake you awake
for school, sometimes
you're grinding your teeth.

You've got an eye
for the orange-flecked salamander hiding
in leafmeal, the one stone amid the gravel heap
that discloses a fossil imprint.

You make mandalas
of fiery and stippled paint. Your people yearn,
with large eyes and hands, taking it all in, reaching out,
hurtling toward the hurts from which I cannot protect you,
and the ones I sometimes inflict.

## II

O giver of gifts, you disarm me
before I know the portcullis is dropping,
you sense it and get in under the wire,
with a hug, or a drawing. You sit in my lap, you snuggle
easily – always comfortable.

Creatively quirky, drawing "The King of Cats and Cows,"
a fierce devil-cat with crown and horns,
spurting milk from its udder,
and a cartoon of a funny-looking man, captioned "This is Joe.
He is very nice, except for when he eats salad."

Working hard at what suits you, but only
when it suits you, able to find
something else that calls you
at just the moment
the chores need doing.

Star of your own show,
funny faces in the mirror,
changing clothes, practicing gestures,
flair and flourish
are your crown and scepter.

When you're tired you lie down to sleep,
not fighting it. Your heart reaches out to animals
with special tenderness. Spiders don't count.
Every possible lair – shoes, clothes dried on the line –
must be checked. By me.

Second son, you know in your bones
that justice is good, achievement commendable
but timing is key;
artful dodger,
parrying sadness with laughter, anger with kisses.

From time to time
out of the clear blue of smiling eyes,
come hugs like your father's when he was alive:
long, generous, sincere.

# THE TERRIBLE QUIET MORNING AFTER THE MEMORIAL SERVICE

FEATURED POET

bereft
you have left me
on this raft
while the river runs
slow swift
singing sad sorrow
murmuring harrow
haunt
fallow want
grief splits me wide

bereft
rolling this ride
by my side
your suns
sad quizzical
young boys
buoyed by life
I their raft
they my gift

*Amelia Williams*

# FOR EEYORE

How your gloom glowed like a lighthouse beam
through every mis-adventure: your tail
taken for a bell-pull, birthday balloon popped,
honey all eaten, dinner thistles
sat upon, tail numbed with cold
for the rescue of baby Roo.
Your lugubrious wisdom endeared you
to every child of disappointment
told "cheer up", "be a good sport."
Without any words yet, for irony, we understood the power
of meeting a moment of injustice with a lofty
phrase, the equipoise of placing the tattered red balloon
into the empty honey jar. "Ha-ha," Eeyore, old chum,
"Merriment and what-not."



*Amelia Williams*

# MY SIDE OF THE WALL

It was typical: I could hear my family talking about me while I listened in. It was a good thing the walls in our house were paper thin, because they did this to me all the time. They talked about my reckless lifestyle, my unfortunate fashion, and the way I sped through life as if I were in a race to find my future before anyone else did. Maybe they were right.

The only problem was that they were still treating me as if I were nine years old, forcing me into another room while they deliberated my fate. Back then I wasn't privy to my own shortcomings, apparently they were selected by my parents and my two older siblings, Seth and Josie.

My family told me that I was a wild child who needed every bit of preventative fencing as possible. Perhaps they were worried I was going to hurt myself. True, I liked to venture down abandoned roads on my bicycle for hours alone. But that didn't mean I wasn't coming back, it just meant that I was coming back on a different day, and usually with various coloured spots from my acts of fearlessness. Then there was the time I skipped two days of high school to go see my favourite rock band with my friends. But that act of independence didn't mean that I disrespected my teachers, it just meant that there was a need for improvement and compromise in my school schedule. It was as simple as that.

But things had changed. Time had changed. I wasn't nine years old or in high school anymore. I had slowed down on the path to my future and had grown up into a woman with cares and responsibilities.

It all happened the year I turned nineteen. The year my world changed forever.

I had taken a year off from life to figure out how I was going to live. It wasn't a particularly foreign concept, but I was determined to pursue it nonetheless.

With so many interests in this world, it was hard for me to narrow down the suspects. I knew that I wanted a university education, to attain a degree in something, but what exactly? I loved astronomy, history and biology—those were the top contenders.

The next step in my mind was to match them against each other and have them battle it out in the boxing ring. Then I would have my answer. Here's how it ended: the Trojans battled the birds and the bees, but then the cosmos blew them both out of the sky. Astronomy it was.

Of course I could only tell my family about my weird little analogies. No one else would understand. My father used to say that I was the perfect blend of nuts and crazy. But I loved him anyway.

I had applied to three different universities, one of them being a local school just a short commute away. I was excited and nervous at the same time. Chamomile tea became a daily tonic to calm my anticipation.

Eagerly I awaited news of my acceptance, harassing the mailman each morning with ruthless smiles until he too gave into my excitement.

Then the day arrived.

I awakened to sound of my mom knocking on my bedroom door.

"Mags, are you awake?"

I could hear myself mouthing the words with a yawn. "Yep. I'm up, Mom."

"Mags, I need to talk to you."

"Come on in, Mom. What's on your mind?"

"Well, Mags," she said opening the door, "we need to talk about your doctor's appointment."

"Uh huh," I slurred, my eyes still closed.

"Maggie, this is serious. Wake up, sweetie."

Although I had been a wild child and the black sheep of the family for the most part, I still loved my mom's terms of endearment for me. I was still the baby of the family and that stood for something, regardless of my unruly past.

There she was however, driven more than ever to save me from myself. A beautiful woman with unwavering support for her baby girl. I loved her for that.

"Maggie, you've taken the initiative to apply to universities and your father and I are very proud of you. You know that, right?"

"Of course, Mom."

"And we are so happy that you've found a stable path to set your goals on."

I watched as a tear dripped down my mother's cheek.

"Mom, why are you crying? I thought you were happy about me doing something positive with my life."

She wiped the tear away with the cuff of her sleeve. "Of course I'm happy for you, Mags. The entire family is."

"Then what's the problem? What's upsetting you?"

My mother was silent.

"Mom, it's okay. I've known about the test results for days. You don't have to tell me."

The tears just poured down her face faster.

"Mom, we were expecting this, remember?"

"I know, Mags, I know."

"So let me deal with this. I know you, Dad, Josie and Seth want to protect me but you have to understand that I'm an adult now. Not telling me first about the results made me feel like a kid again, on my side of the wall."

"Is that how you knew?"

"Yes, Mom—that's how I knew. You all had a family meeting while I listened on the other side of the wall. You never realized that I could hear everything—the walls are very thin."

"Mags, it's just...that...we didn't know how to tell you. Your father answered the phone; he was the one who spoke to the doctor. We didn't know that you were listening."

I smiled at my mother. "This is *my* future we're talking about, correct?"

I watched as she nodded in agreement.

Did she finally understand? Had it really taken this long for her to realize that her little girl was now a woman in search of control?

"Mom, that's why I wanted a new future—something I could believe in. I've always been the free spirit of the family. I climbed trees, broke lots of bones, took lots of risks. I can handle this. Out of everyone in our family, I was meant to have this because I'm the one who takes chances. My life has already been full of surprises and accidents—this is just another hurdle."

"Maggie, we just want to take care of you, make sure that you're safe. But I guess that's not up to us anymore, is it?"

I shook my head, looking into her eyes.

"Mom, I'm not a kid anymore. I will always be your baby but I'm not a kid anymore."

"Okay, then. Why don't you tell me more about the universities you've applied to," she smiled, wiping away another tear. "I want to hear more about your studies."

So there we sat on my childhood bed talking about dreams, goals, life and the future. It was a conversation I would remember forever.

Throughout the following week, I fretted. I waited for the postman each day, anxious for a letter of acceptance, dreading the possibility that all three universities would turn me down.

I found myself looking for any sort of physical distraction. I rode my bike, went shopping, cleaned the house many times over, and hiked through the nearby park as much as possible. It felt great to get my mind off of my impending future. I even spent hours just sitting on the swings in the neighbourhood park my parents used to take me to as a kid. Back and forth I moved, floating through the air, my thoughts escaping any looming letters or results.

Then Thursday came along.

I was lying on the sofa in the family room, watching an episode of *I Dream of Jeannie* on the television, when the doorbell rang. I stood up and slowly made my way into the hallway, toward the front door. And that's when it hit me: this was it!

I could see the mailman through the window beside the door. He was grinning.

At that moment I heard Seth running for the door. "I got it," he said gliding past me. "Sorry Mags, I'm waiting for something. It's supposed to arrive today."

He must have seen my disfigured expression for he notably stated "What's with the narly face? I won't hog the mail, kiddo. Relax."

Seth opened the door and exchanged pleasantries with the mailman as I looked on from the hallway. It was then that I felt a wave of nerves overcome me and I couldn't bring myself to step any further.

Unfortunately, that was the last thing I remembered. After that moment, things changed. The future that I had so desperately sought, revolted and turned on me. This life of mine was headed in a new direction—one that I had not desired nor intended.

My life darkened. A weird, unfamiliar noise was heard in the background. It sounded like a single string of a violin being played. It was eerie and siren-like.

Above me I could see a mass of stars, guiding my body onto a new path. As I passed by them I realized what they were doing. Each twinkling light was acting as a protective rail, surrounding me, keeping me balanced but allowing me to move forward.

Each step I took, felt heavy, as if my legs were being pulled from the earth like a tree. Ahead of me I saw blackened sky. Adventurous as I was, there was now something inside of me holding me back. I understood fear for the first time.

There was a grievous feeling in my heart as I felt a shadow of pain slowly pass over my body. Then I felt nothing. And for the longest time I remained still.

I had many questions but I was alone with only my thoughts and no answers.

The anticipation of my future had pushed me into a trance, intoxicating me with feelings I had not bargained for. Perhaps the weight of my scholastic destiny was too much for me to bear. A reaction like this did seem a little dramatic especially to a harmless letter designed of paper and ink. But it was a natural reaction, unscripted and honest.

I listened carefully to my surroundings and that's when I heard a voice. It was familiar, and gentle. It was Seth. The pitch in his throat revealed his concern. Had he accidentally opened one of my letters instead of his? I would have to kill him if he did—I had been waiting for those letters for months now. I tried to listen to what he was saying, but his speech was blurred. That brother of mine, he probably opened my letters on purpose just so that he could read them first.

Then I heard a woman's voice, very faint.

"Can she hear us?"

Hmm...a female voice talking down to me—it could only be my sister Josie. I bet she was in on it too, trying to steal my thunder, opening my letters before me. Strange siblings of mine.

Why couldn't the members of my family just leave my personal life alone? That would be a question for another time perhaps. Right now I just had to focus.

"She was accepted," I heard another voice say. And I knew right away that it was my mother. But for some reason her voice seemed different. In fact, all of their voices seemed different.

"One of those happy days," a male voice returned.

It was my dad, he was here too.

"I was accepted?" I shouted in excitement. "Yes! Seth—it's okay. I'm not mad at you for opening my letters. I can't believe it—I'm going to school. I'm going to have a future after all!"

"She deserved it," Josie said. "Mags worked hard to get into school. She finally got her act together. What unbelievable timing."

"Josie, Josie—aren't you proud of me? I'm going to school!"

There was no reply. I was wondering what had happened to the excited state of my family. But now there was only silence.

"Aren't you all happy for me?"

But still, no sound.

"This is a positive step for me, isn't it wonderful?"

No answer. Nothing.

"Isn't anyone listening to me? I can hear you, can't you hear me?"

Then I realized that it was just like when I was kid and the rest of the family was on the other side of the wall. But there was no getting over this wall.

Life is a funny thing. Just when you think you've got a handle on it, you lose your grip. For me, it was no longer a time of defiance. It was a time of acceptance. It was a hard concept for me to understand as I, up until this point, had embraced life with physical extreme. But now I understood limitations.

For months, my family came to the hospital to visit me in my state of rest. Over time they watched as my body slowly deteriorated from the leukemia that had taken over this life. At first I could hear their voices, but gradually they faded to silence. As it turned out, my future was governed by something I could not fight nor wrestle nor defeat.

This wall could not be breached, but finally I was at peace on my side of it.

# MERCURY IN RETROGRADE

When the hairs on my arm
—normally as responsive
as your fingers
late night channel flicking—
don't stand quite as stiff
when lips
run across my shoulder blades.

The pump of my heart
—so often as vigorous
as back alley bull frogs
waking us after a downpour—
softens slightly
at the interlocking of fingers
under Sunday morning sheets.

Palms caressing eyelids
—intended to soothe
and reverse a week
bookended by rush hour traffic—
make daybreak shadows
on cedar floors appear
a little more grey.

A coffee slurp,
a pen's click-tap-click-repeat
(three down is not that hard!)
causes a frustrated sigh,
which goes unnoticed!
sparking a second that ripples
across a newspaper corner.

Mercury is in retrograde until
—at some undefined point
(possibly a Sunday morning?)—
pillow drool sprinkled with bagel
crumbs and grey strays
transition back into natural orbit,
give me a smile,
make my bull frog heart
croak once more.

*Mitchell Noel Kelly*

# BIOGRAPHIES

## KARA BARTLEY

Kara Bartley graduated in 2005 with a master's degree in Vertebrate Palaeontology from the University at Buffalo. She started writing her first novel, "The Siamese Mummy", while on a dig in Kansas, where she unearthed not only bones, but storylines as well. Since then, she has written and self-published three other books, her most recent being "The Moon In Habock's Mirror", a teen-driven, time-traveling fantasy novel. You can visit her online at: www.theivoryowl.com or www.karabartley.blogspot.com.

## JULIE CORBETT

Julie L Corbett writes poetry and takes photographs. Julie is also an active member of the spoken word community in Hull and the East Riding of Yorkshire. Her poetry has been published in Fib Review, The Right Eyed Deer, Unfold, and Incandescent as well as a number of anthologies. Her forthcoming chapbook Reading the Humber from Folded Word Press will be available in spring 2012.

## TRACY DAVIDSON

Tracy Davidson enjoys writing poetry and flash fiction. Her work has appeared in various publications including Modern Haiku, Mslexia, Atlas Poetica, A Hundred Gourds and Notes from the Gean. In 2011 she won the Winchester Writers Conference Haiku competition. She lives in a quiet village in Warwickshire, England with her mad Miniature Schnauzer (and no, that is not a euphemism!).

## ELIZABETH DONNELLY

Elizabeth Donnelly is in her 40s and lives in the UK, where she is currently between homes. She would never describe herself as a writer, but will push herself to type a few words onto a screen when there's a deadline in the offing.

Still trying to find her voice and reading a lot of books because good writers need to read before they write, Elizabeth thinks the great novel within her may eventually be written when she's 87.

## ANTHONY KANE EVANS

Anthony Kane Evans has had over forty short stories published in various UK/US/Australian literary magazines and anthologies, including *London Magazine, Orbis, Æsthetica, The Tusculum Review, Pear Noir* and *Etchings*. He also has a story in an upcoming issue of *Wet Ink* (March 2012).

He's British but lives in Copenhagen. He is currently trying to interest an agent in a comic novel called 'Kwakman.'

## MARILYN FRANCIS

Marilyn Francis lives and works in Midsomer Norton in the wild south west of England. Her first poetry collection, *red silk slippers,* (Circaidy Gregory Press, 2009) was said to, 'deftly dissect the quotidian' - she's still trying to work out what that might mean.

## JESSE GADSBY

Jesse Gadsby was born in Victoria but now lives in the small town of Agassiz in British Columbia. He has been writing since the age of twelve and is in the process of completing two novels. An anthology of poems as well as several short stories is in the works. When he isn't writing he flips burgers to pay the bills and occasionally entertains friends with his boundless wit.

## FRANCIS HAYES

Francis Hayes was born in the south of England. At the age of 19 he went to university in the north of England to study law. He remained in the north, working as a lawyer in local government.

In 1997 he was offered the opportunity to retire at the age of fifty to help his employers save money. He has seen no evidence that it worked for them but it certainly worked for him.

When not writing he does glass enamelling, making jewellery and ornaments that he sells in craft fairs in North Yorkshire.

## MICHAEL LEE JOHNSON

Michael Lee Johnson is a poet, and editor, from Itasca, Illinois who lived 10 years in Canada during the Vietnam era, published in 24 countries. He runs five poetry sites, his website: http://poetryman.mysite.com. His published poetry books are available through his website above, Amazon.Com, Borders Books, iUniverse and Lulu.com:
*http://www.lulu.com/spotlight/promomanusa.*

## MITCHELL NOEL KELLY

Mitchell has had a handful of short stories, flash fiction and poetry published across North America, Asia and Australia. He currently lives in Melbourne, Australia where he was admitted as a lawyer in late 2011, though he vows never to let a legal career get in the way of his love of writing.

## MAUDE LARKE

Maude Larke lives in France. She has come back to creative writing after years in the university system, analyzing others' texts, and to classical music as an ardent amateur, after fifteen years of piano and voice in her youth. Publications include *Bird's Eye reView, Naugatuck River Review, Oberon, Cyclamens and Swords, riverbabble* and *Sketchbook.*

## TOM PESCATORE

Tom Pescatore grew up outside Philadelphia, he is an active member of the growing punk/lit scene within the city and hopes to spread the word on Philadelphia's new poets. He maintains a poetry blog: amagicalmistake.blogspot.com. His work has been published in literary magazines both nationally and internationally but he'd rather have them carved on the Walt Whitman bridge or on the sidewalks of Philadelphia's old Skid Row.

## BOB SMITH

Bob Smith (not a nom de plume, just uncreative parents – he has a brother Joe) is a Canadian writer who has published three novels and has had short stories appear in ezines, newspapers, and anthologies. Settings as diverse as children's camps from Lebanon to British Columbia and Ontario colleges from Hamilton to Haliburton have exposed him to incredibly varied people, a rich source of inspiration for his writing.

## E. RUSSELL SMITH

E. Russell Smith was born in Toronto, was educated in Montreal, Cambridge, and elsewhere, and has been a teacher and writer. In this latter capacity he produced two novels, two collections of stories, two collections of poetry, one ecology field study and countless inclusions in lit mags, journals and newspapers here and there. Presently he writes only poetry and personal correspondence, mainly for his own satisfaction, and is reading the poetry of D. H. Lawrence. His poems have twice been selected as Poems of the Year by the Inter Board Poetry Community (IBPC). He anticipates the appearance of a new collection from The Right Eyed Deer Press in early 2012, and Toronto readings at the Rowers Pub series on Monday May 7, 2012, and at the Art Bar Poetry Series on Tuesday May 8, 2012. He lives in Ottawa, Ont. Canada.

## CONNAL VICKERS

Connal has been writing stories for years but has only recently got around to finishing them. He was a journalist once but real life took over and he moved through a number of jobs from fisherman to hot dog machine salesman and most recently worked as a carpenter and cabinet maker. He now writes full time, a decision which will terrify his bank manager when he hears of it.

## AMELIA WILLIAMS

Amelia L. Williams, PhD, is a poet, cook, soccer mom, hiker and medical writer living intentional community in the foothills of the Blue Ridge Mountains. Her recent accomplishments include hosting a World Café and learning how Twitter can be useful.

Her poem "Lane Shift" appeared in Issue 5 of Hospital Drive: A Journal of Word & Image (http://hospitaldrive.med.virginia.edu.). She has participated in poetry readings at Writer House in Charlottesville and Rapunzel's Coffee and Books in Lovingston.

www.ingramcontent.com/pod-product-compliance
Ingram Content Group UK Ltd.
Pitfield, Milton Keynes, MK11 3LW, UK
UKHW051135260726
13967UKWH00010B/3069

9 781105 614422